To:

From:

'TWAS THE NIGHT BEFORE CHRISTMAS ON THE FARM

words by Craig Manning
pictures by Sumi Collina

sourcebooks
wonderland

'Twas the night before Christmas, and all 'round the farm
Not a creature was stirring, tucked in safe and warm.

The stockings were hung on each barn door with care.
The animals hoped soon St. Nick would be there.

The cows had stopped mooing, the horses weren't neighing,
The cats weren't meowing, the donkeys weren't braying.
Sheep and pigs were all snuggled away in their beds,
While visions of Christmas Day danced in their heads.

All of a sudden, a sound filled the air,

Giving a lamb in the barn quite the scare.

"What was that?!" she asked, though no one else heard.

Despite the great noise, no one even stirred!

The lamb got out of bed, and she crept toward the door
To see what the cold winter's night had in store.
She perked up her ears and glanced out at the snow.
At first, she saw nothing but the moon all aglow.

When, what to her wandering eyes should appear,
But an object in flight, and coming quite near!
"It's a bird!" the lamb thought, for what else could fly?
She'd never seen something else soar through the sky.

It came closer and closer but wasn't a bird!

For no bird she knew makes the jingles she heard!

It looked like a tractor, big and metal and red,

With a herd of eight creatures just flying ahead.

Much faster than eagles these strange animals flew,
And from there in the barn, the lamb heard a voice too:
"Now, Dasher! Now, Dancer! Now, Prancer and Vixen!
On, Comet! On, Cupid! On, Donner and Blitzen!"

The strange party had landed atop the farmhouse,

And the lamb watched in awe, sitting still as a mouse.

Just what could it be? She still didn't know.

But she had a few thoughts as she gazed through the snow:

This large tractor seemed odd and was painted bright red,
Where the farmer's was usually bright green instead.
"And don't tractors have wheels?" the little lamb thought.
This tractor could fly, but the farmer's could not!

Those creatures must be horses up there on the roof.

They were prancing and pawing with each little hoof.

But the lamb saw each horse had big horns on its head.
"All the horses I know don't *have* horns," the lamb said.

And what of the man with the red coat so merry
With pink, rosy cheeks and a nose like a cherry?
His hair was bright white, and he had a round belly
That shook when he laughed, like a bowl full of jelly

Those weren't the clothes that the farmer would wear.

Plus, the farmer was lean with a head of dark hair!

The lamb was confused. Just *who* could it be?

'Til she heard, "Ho, ho, ho," and was starting to see...

The man climbed the chimney so lively and quick.

Then the lamb finally knew—oh, it must be St. Nick!

Santa was here! That's who this must be!

"He's bringing presents for all, and maybe for me."

And then all made sense, as clear as the day:

This wasn't a tractor. It was Santa's sleigh!

And the horses with horns? Well, it would appear,

Weren't horses at all, but Santa's reindeer!

The cows were still sleeping, and a pig gave a snore
As Santa appeared at the barn's open door.
The lamb tried to hide. What *would* Santa think?
But the old man just smiled, and gave a quick wink.

He spoke not a word, and his work took a while.

He filled the farm stockings, then turned with a smile.

And then, just like magic, Santa was gone!

Back up on the roof as the night turned to dawn.

He sprung to his sleigh, gave his team a short whistle,
And away they all flew, like the down of a thistle.
Then the lamb heard a shout, as they drove out of sight—
"Merry Christmas to all, and to all a good night!"

"For Jillian, who loves Christmas almost as much as she loves cats."

—CM

"To Morgana, Oli and Feri, my little lambs"

—SC

All book illustrations have been sketched and colored in Photoshop with a Wacom Intuos tablet.

Published by Sourcebooks Wonderland, an imprint of Sourcebooks Kids

P.O. Box 4410, Naperville, Illinois 60567-4410
(630) 961-3900
sourcebookskids.com
Library of Congress Cataloging-in-Publication Data is on file with the publisher.

Source of Production: 1010 Printing Asia Limited, North Point, Hong Kong, China
Date of Production: May 2020
Run Number: 5018888

Printed and bound in China.
OGP 10 9 8 7 6 5 4 3 2 1